Book 10

Glam Opening!

JILL SANTOPOLO

Aladdin
NEW YORK LONDON TORONTO SYDNEY NEW DELHI

ALADDIN
An imprint of Simon & Schuster Children's Publishing Division
1230 Avenue of the Americas, New York, NY 10020
First Aladdin paperback edition June 2017

Also available in an Aladdin hardcover edition.

For information about special discounts for bulk purchases, please contact
Simon & Schuster Special Sales at 1-866-506-1949 or business@simonandschuster.com.
The Simon & Schuster Speakers Bureau can bring authors to your live event. For more information or to book an event, contact the Simon & Schuster Speakers Bureau at 1-866-248-3049 or visit our website at www.simonspeakers.com.
Series design by Jeanine Henderson
Cover design by Laura Lyn DiSiena
The text of this book was set in Adobe Caslon.
Manufactured in the United States of America 0517 OFF
10 9 8 7 6 5 4 3 2 1
Library of Congress Control Number 2017931082
ISBN 978-1-4814-6396-6 (hc)
ISBN 978-1-4814-6395-9 (pbk)
ISBN 978-1-4814-6397-3 (eBook)

Glam Opening!

* . * * . * * . * *

Also by Jill Santopolo

Sparkle Spa

Book 1: All That Glitters

Book 2: Purple Nails and Puppy Tails

Book 3: Makeover Magic

Book 4: True Colors

Book 5: Bad News Nails

Book 6: A Picture-Perfect Mess

Book 7: Bling It On!

Book 8: Wedding Bell Blues

Book 9: Fashion Disaster

For Marie, Eliot, Marianna, and Anne,
who have been on this sparkly journey with me
since the very beginning

With many glittery thanks to Karen and Miriam,
and to all the dazzling people at Simon & Schuster
and DeFiore & Co.

Contents

Glam Opening!

* . * * . * * . * *

one

Ruby Red Slippers

"Munchkins, you can come over here with me!" Aly Tanner's younger sister, Brooke, was standing on top of a teal pedicure chair. "Sophie and I have all the brightest colors!"

Aly was glad that Brooke was dealing with the Munchkins. The Flying Monkeys were on the opposite side of the Sparkle Spa, right near where Sparkly, the girls' dog, was sleeping. They were looking at darker nail polish colors with Lily. And Charlotte was standing at the door with her twin brother, Caleb. She was checking names off the appointment list, and he was handling "security." Caleb didn't always help out at the Sparkle Spa, but once in a while, when the girls thought the salon would be extra crowded, they asked him to stand by the door to make sure there weren't too many people coming into the salon at once. Today was the most crowded day Aly could remember.

She kept looking at the sign on the wall, the new one a man from the health department had put up last week. It said: OCCUPANCY BY MORE THAN 16 PEOPLE IS UNLAWFUL. There was a similar sign hanging right outside the Sparkle Spa, in Aly and Brooke's mom's salon, True Colors, but there you were allowed to have fifty people. If the girls and their mom didn't obey the signs, the health department could close their salons—maybe even forever.

Aly counted: six Sparkle Spa workers, five Munchkins, and four Flying Monkeys. Luckily,

Sparkly didn't count, according to the health department, since he was a dog.

"Caleb," Aly said, walking over to the door, "we're only allowed one more person in the spa."

He nodded. "I've been keeping track," he answered.

While Aly was standing there, Jenica Posner came in from True Colors. "Hey," she said. "Looks super-busy in there."

Aly tucked her sweaty bangs behind her ear. "Yes," she said. "Because the second- and third-grade play is *The Wizard of Oz*, a bunch of the Munchkins and Flying Monkeys wanted to get their nails done before tomorrow's performance."

"And they all want to stay to see how everyone else's manicure looks?" Jenica guessed.

"Exactly," Aly told her.

Jenica Posner was the coolest girl in all of Auden Elementary. She was the captain of the sixth grade girls' soccer team, the Auden Angels, and was one of the main reasons that Aly and Brooke were allowed to start the Sparkle Spa in the first place. One day when True Colors was extra busy, Mom let Aly give Jenica a rainbow sparkle pedicure. Jenica scored a ton of goals in her next soccer game, and before long all the Angels wanted rainbow sparkle pedicures.

True Colors couldn't fit them into its daily appointments, so Aly and Brooke were able to start their own salon, the Sparkle Spa, in the spare back room of their mom's salon. There were lots of rules the girls had to follow, but they'd been doing a great job, and their salon had been open for almost the whole school year. The Angels still came by for rainbow sparkle pedicures every Tuesday, but sometimes Jenica stopped by to say hello when her nana was getting a manicure in True Colors.

"Your mom's salon is pretty crowded today too," Jenica said, stepping into the Sparkle Spa.

"Bridal party," Aly said. "In addition to regulars. And the health department came by yesterday to give us these signs about how many people could be in each space. You're the very last person who can be in the Sparkle Spa right now, until someone leaves. You're number sixteen."

"Wow," Jenica said. "You'd better get some of these Munchkins out of here."

Aly nodded. "I should probably start doing some manicures."

"Sounds good," Jenica said. "At least when the Angels come, we don't stay too much past our drying time!" Then she turned and headed back into True Colors.

Charlotte tapped Aly's shoulder. "Clementine's ready for you. She's a Munchkin and she wants polka dots." She handed Aly two bottles of polish: Ruby Red Slippers and Yellow Submarine.

Aly took them and then walked over to the manicure station, where Clementine Stern, a second grader, was waiting.

"Congratulations on being a Munchkin," Aly told her.

"I'm really excited," Clementine said. "I really wanted the part of Toto, but then I found out that you can't get that part unless you're a real dog. So now I get to do 'Follow the Yellow Brick Road,' and I'm in the Lollipop Guild."

"That's pretty awesome," Aly said. "When I was in second grade, our play was *Mary Poppins*. I was a chimney sweep. Munchkins get much better costumes than chimney sweeps. So red dots on yellow, or yellow dots on red?"

"Red on yellow," Clementine answered.

"You got it." Aly put some polish remover on a cotton ball and started removing Clementine's old polish.

She was so caught up in the manicure, she didn't notice that even though some people had left, more Munchkins, along with Glinda the Good Witch and the Wicked Witch of the West, had arrived.

"Brooke, Aly!" Caleb called. "We need you."

Aly and Brooke hurried over, telling their customers they'd be right back.

"What's going on?" Brooke said, pushing her glasses up on her nose as she got to the door.

"This," Charlotte said, pointing into True Colors.

Four girls were waiting by the door to get into the Sparkle Spa.

Six grown-ups were in waiting-for-a-manicure chairs.

Eight grown-ups were waiting for drying-after-a-manicure chairs.

Three grown-ups were standing near the reception desk.

And that didn't count all the people Mom's manicurists were working on. Or the manicurists themselves!

"We already have sixteen people in the Sparkle Spa, and there's not even a place to tell them to wait in your mom's salon!"

Just as Aly was checking out the situation, Mrs. Tanner, the girls' mom, came over.

"Brooke, Aly," she said, "your customers can't overflow into True Colors. I'm bumping up against my fifty-person limit, and I can't have them in here."

"We're *at* our limit!" Brooke wailed. "I hate the health department!"

Mom closed her eyes for a moment. "I'm not a superfan of their new signs either," she began, slowly opening her eyes. "But it's important to follow their rules, because they keep our customers safe—and if we don't follow the law, they could shut us down. I trust you girls will figure this out."

"We just need more *space*," Brooke said. "If we had more space, we could have more people, and if we had more people, it wouldn't be a problem. But the Sparkle Spa is really small compared to everything else in the world, except for maybe my closet. And no one can run a business out of a closet anyway."

Aly couldn't help but smile. Brooke made her smile all the time. She wasn't sure if it was because Brooke was in third grade and Aly was in fifth, but Aly sometimes found the way Brooke's brain worked to be funny.

"We'll fix it, Mom," Aly said. "Don't worry."

"Thank you," Mom said. "But I hear you about the space, Brookie. I could use more too."

"What are we going to *do*?" Brooke asked Aly.

Aly sighed. There seemed like only one obvious answer. "We're going to have to tell people who have dry manicures to leave. And that they can meet their friends next door at the Men's Shoe Shack."

"The Men's Shoe Shack?" Brooke repeated, scrunching up her face.

Aly shrugged. "There's never anyone in there anyway. They can wait out front on the bench there."

It was true: Almost every time the girls passed by the Men's Shoe Shack, which was probably about ten times a week, hardly anyone was inside buying shoes.

"Okay," Brooke agreed. "The Men's Shoe Shack it is!"

When the sisters went back to the Sparkle Spa, Aly stood on a pedicure chair and explained the situation. Anyone whose nails were already dry had to leave, and she and Brooke suggested they meet in front of the Men's Shoe Shack.

There were lots of grumbles and "No fairs" coming from the Munchkins and Flying Monkeys. Aly sent her sister a Secret Sister Eye Message: *Help! What do we do now?*

Brooke smiled and then quickly jumped up next to Aly and said, "And whoever tells us the name of the silliest-looking shoe in the front window gets an extra-special surprise pedicure from me next time you come to the Sparkle Spa!"

That did it. Everyone wanted the extra-special pedicure, so three Munchkins and one Flying Monkey headed out the door. Caleb and Charlotte told the four girls waiting by the door leading to True Colors that they could come inside, and everything calmed down for a moment.

But Aly knew it was only for a moment. She also knew that the play was a special case and they didn't *always* have this many kids wanting to come to the

Sparkle Spa at once . . . but there had been more and more special cases recently. Enough that Aly knew they'd have to figure out a plan. What could they do about finding more space?

two

Blue Skies

The next morning, Aly and Brooke were getting ready to head to Auden Elementary, even though it was a Saturday. They decided they couldn't miss watching their clients perform in *The Wizard of Oz.*

"I'm still surprised you didn't want to be in the show, Brookester," Aly said. Since Brooke was in third grade, she could've tried out for any part she wanted. "Lily and Charlotte and I had fun being chimney sweeps two years ago. Even if the costumes weren't great."

Brooke shrugged as she snapped a clip with

sparkly streamers into her hair. "I like saying my own words, not words other people tell me to say."

Aly laughed. Her sister certainly did like to talk a lot, and Aly had never considered that being onstage meant you had to say someone else's words. She could understand why Brooke wouldn't like that.

"Anyway," Brooke said, "this way I get to polish everyone's nails and then cheer for them and be a part of the show in two ways—as a polisher and a cheerer. And two ways is better than one way."

That made sense to Aly. "Do you want to go to True Colors after the show?" she asked. Because of their mom's rules, the Sparkle Spa was only allowed to be open three days a week—two school days and one weekend day—so the girls usually had the spa open on Sundays, Tuesdays, and Fridays, unless there was a special request.

That meant that Saturdays were free days. Sometimes the girls went to the park, sometimes they hung out with friends, sometimes they went places with their dad, and sometimes they went to True Colors to help out. They refilled rhinestone bags for the manicurists, reorganized the polish wall when it got messy, straightened up the magazines, and talked to the regular customers while their nails were drying.

"I don't know," Brooke said. "It's been *so* crowded. And we'll be adding to the people count. And what if there are too many? Then we'd have to hide in the Sparkle Spa with no customers, and that's a little bit boring. I mean, we could do each other's nails, I guess, like in the old days, but maybe we can figure out something else to do today."

"I guess you're right," Aly agreed. Her sister did make a lot of sense.

Aly and Brooke were about to head downstairs for breakfast when their mom poked her head into their room. "Brookie, I heard what you said, and there's something else you could do this afternoon. How about you girls come with me to look at different new spaces for True Colors?"

"A *new* space for True Colors?" Brooke asked, just as Aly said, "And for the Sparkle Spa too?"

"Yes and yes," Mom said. "Our current space is too small. I want a salon that can fit at least sixty-five people, not fifty. And I want you girls to be able to fit at least twenty-five people, not sixteen. I talked it over with Dad last night, and this is the answer that makes the most sense. We need to expand."

"Wow," both girls said.

"I have so many ideas," Brooke added. "About what we could have at the new Sparkle Spa."

But Aly stopped listening. She was already making a list in her head of what they should look for in a new space:

- *A big, big area for True Colors, and a bigger-than-they-had-now area for the Sparkle Spa*
- *Within walking distance from school (like TC and SS were now)*
- *Windows facing the street (which was good for attracting customers)*
- *On the ground floor (for the same reason)*
- *Really pretty and bright (because when places were pretty and bright, people liked being inside them)*

Aly thought that was a great list. She would tell Brooke about it later and see if there was anything to add.

Later that morning, the Auden auditorium was packed for the show. Besides Brooke and Aly's friends, lots of other kids were there too, along with parents and grandparents.

Aly was very impressed with the show. It wasn't the whole *Wizard of Oz*, just the greatest hits—the songs most everyone knew. The music teacher, Mr. Mehta, explained this before the show started, but the performers had costumes and were singing and dancing. It was pretty awesome.

"Look at our manicures!" Brooke squealed when the Munchkins came onstage. "Don't they look wonderful?"

Aly thought they did. They made the stage look even brighter.

Of course the girls wanted to stay for the after-the-show celebration, but with their mom waiting for their business date, they hurried off.

The first place they saw was a former coat store, right next door to the bridal shop where the girls got their dresses for the wedding of their mom's best friend—and best manicurist!—Joan. There were still some coatracks in there, and signs on the walls advertising "Kids' Denim Jackets!" and "Womens' Raincoats!" Aly wasn't surprised that the coat store had gone out of business, because where the Tanners lived, it was pretty warm all year round. That's why people always wanted pedicures. The coat store space was big, but Aly wasn't sure if it was much bigger than the space True Colors was in now.

"What do you think, Mom?" she asked.

Mom was walking around the store, talking to the woman who owned the building. She was asking about the plumbing. Aly hadn't even thought about the plumbing, but they'd need more pedicure sinks, which meant lots of pipes carrying water. Aly added that to the list in her head.

Good plumbing.

"Well," the building owner said, "you're welcome to renovate, if you'd like, but there's no plumbing other than in the restroom."

"Oh," Mom said. "I see."

She walked back to Aly and Brooke. "I have a feeling this isn't the right space for us," she said.

Aly and Brooke nodded.

"Not enough windows, anyway," Brooke said. "We need a brighter space so everyone can see the beautiful nail polish colors."

The second place they visited was gorgeous—huge and bright—with windows on two sides, since it was a corner building. It had been a hair salon, so there was plumbing. And it was decorated in white and silver with a Blue Skies trim. It was really pretty, as far as Aly was concerned.

"I love this one!" Brooke said as they walked in.

"It does look promising," Mom said. While Mom was touring and asking questions, Aly and Brooke headed toward a back corner. There was a window on one side and a wall on the other.

"If Mom rents this space, do you think we could get a window in the Sparkle Spa?" Brooke asked.

"Maybe," Aly said. She thought about how cool that would be. Right now, the Sparkle Spa didn't have any windows. Just a door that led to the Dumpster behind True Colors.

"Girls?" Mom said, from the door of the shop. "Let's go."

"What was wrong with that one?" Aly asked. "It seemed perfect."

Mom sighed. "It was great, but much too expensive. True Colors is doing well, but not that well. We can't afford that place."

The third location the girls went into wasn't as small as the first one or as big as the second one. It had windows on one side of the building and it used to be an ice-cream shop. So while it didn't have the kind of plumbing they needed, it did have *some* plumbing they could easily make work for the salon, Mom said.

"We probably won't get a window here," Brooke whispered.

"Probably not," Aly said. She looked around and tried to figure out where the Sparkle Spa could go. Maybe in the area where the ice-cream freezer was? That was a pretty big space. As long as Mom could figure out a way to make it warm in there.

Once Mrs. Tanner took another quick walk around, she told the woman who owned the building, "This looks great. I need to run some things by my bank, but I should be able to make an offer soon."

"You'd better make it fast," the woman said. "Because some other people have been looking at this space and have said the same thing. A coffee shop, a cupcakery, and a juice bar. I need all my offers by today at four."

* * * * *

Back home, while their mom was on the phone with the bank, the girls wrote a list of everything they wanted in the new Sparkle Spa:

- Four pedicure chairs (instead of two)
- Four real manicure stations
- A couch for waiting (not just pillows)
- A bigger polish wall
- Drying chairs separate from the waiting couch

"Oh, and don't forget a desk for us to use for our homework!" Brooke said.

"Couldn't forget that," Aly said, and added it to the list. Then Aly looked at her watch—it was 4:03. "It's past the deadline," she said. "Let's go downstairs and ask Mom if she got the store."

Aly knew the answer before she even asked. Their

mother was sitting at the kitchen table, staring out the window.

"Bad news, girls," she said when she saw Aly and Brooke. "I couldn't get the paperwork in on time, and the other businesses did. A coffee shop's going to move into that space. So we're back to the beginning."

Mom sighed.

Aly sighed.

Brooke sighed.

Actually, though, Aly was secretly a little glad that the ice-cream space didn't work—she was worried about having the Sparkle Spa in a freezer. But she still hoped they'd find a new place soon.

three
White Out

At school on Monday, Aly sat with Charlotte at their lunch table. Lily was a buyer that day instead of a bringer, so she was on the lunch line, waiting to get chicken fingers with french fries and applesauce. Mom had packed Aly's lunch—a cheese sandwich, a pear, pretzels, a little bottle of water, and a chocolate kiss—and Charlotte had lunch from home too. Her mom had different ideas about food than Aly's mom, so Charlotte's lunch had cookies, along with a sandwich made out of peanut butter and marshmallow fluff that was the exact color of White Out nail polish. There were some raisins too, but Aly suspected Charlotte wasn't going to eat those, and a fruit punch juice box.

When Lily sat down, Suzy Davis followed her, dropping into the empty seat across from Aly. Aly and Suzy Davis had a long history of not liking each other, but recently they'd started becoming friendlier—because of two things: (1) Aly and Brooke's favorite manicurist, Joan, married Suzy's uncle, and (2) Suzy helped the girls win a carnival competition by adding her makeup business, Suzy's Spectacular Makeup, to their Sparkle Spa booth. The thing about Suzy was that she was basically a good person, and was really smart, too, but sometimes the way she said things or the way she acted made people upset with her. Aly tried to see past that. Charlotte had a little more trouble. Lily too, but not as much as Charlotte.

"So did your mom find a new place for True Colors?" Lily asked as she opened up her carton of milk.

Aly swallowed a bite of her cheese sandwich. "She found a place, but then someone else rented it to open a coffee shop."

"I hate coffee shops!" Charlotte declared.

Suzy looked at her. "Why?" she asked.

Charlotte's eyes shot daggers at Suzy. "Because they took over the space Aly's mom wanted for True Colors," she said. "Duh."

"That's a dumb reason to hate coffee shops," Suzy said. "That was just one coffee shop, not, like, every coffee shop on earth."

"She's being *supportive*," Lily said, picking up a chicken nugget. "You should try it sometime."

Aly shook her head. As always, Suzy wasn't wrong, she just didn't say what she was thinking in the very nicest way possible. But Lily sounded kind of mean too.

"Anyway," Aly said, "there was another space that was really cool. Brooke and I liked it even better. It was huge and beautiful and used to be a hair salon, but it was too expensive. It's too bad, because the Sparkle Spa could've gotten a window."

"A window?" Charlotte squealed. "For our own signs and stuff?"

Aly shrugged. "Probably. But it's not going to happen." Still, Aly couldn't help dreaming about how cool the Sparkle Spa would look with its very own window.

"I think your mom should get the bigger space so that I can have room there for my makeup business," Suzy said. "People liked it so much at the carnival. And it's not fair, because my mom's company is only online, so I can't have a part of her shop like you and Brooke do with your mom's."

"What did you just say?" Aly asked. Ideas were already starting to spin like a Ferris wheel in Aly's brain.

"People liked my business?" Suzy said.

"No, the other part." Aly put down the pretzel she was about to eat.

"That I should be allowed to have my makeup business in True Colors?" Suzy asked.

"Yes!" Aly answered. "What if another business helps my mom pay her rent? Then she could afford the larger space, and divide some of it with the other business!"

"And still have a window for the Sparkle Spa!" Lily added, punctuating her sentence by stabbing a french fry in the air.

"Exactly!" Aly said. "That's a great idea, Suzy."

"That wasn't her idea," Charlotte said through a mouthful of cookie.

"It actually wasn't," Suzy agreed. "I just wanted a place where I could have Suzy's Spectacular Makeup."

"Okay, fine," Aly said. "It wasn't totally your idea, but it helped give me that idea. I can't wait to tell my mom. I think it'll change everything!"

That night, at dinner, Aly spoke to her mom about the idea.

Mom leaned back in her seat. "That's actually kind of brilliant."

Aly smiled. It was really nice when her mom thought she was smart about something, mostly because Aly thought her mom was the smartest woman she knew.

Brooke was shoveling stir-fry into her mouth, then stopped with a forkful of vegetables halfway to her lips. "Joan's cookies!" she said. "Joan could have a place for her cookie business!"

Joan, in addition to being the girls' favorite manicurist, Suzy Davis's aunt by marriage, and their mom's best friend, was also the best cookie baker the girls knew. Sometimes people asked her to make cookies for parties, and she often made cookies for fun to bring into the salon. She always saved some for Aly and Brooke and their friends, and asked them to give her a report on how they tasted. She even taught the girls how to make sparkly rainbow-colored cookies called Unicorn Treats. Well, originally they were called Unicorn Poop, but Aly thought that was gross, so they changed the name.

"I think Joan is happy running her side business out of her house," Mom said. "But there are a lot of companies that might fit nicely with True Colors. Maybe someone who wants to sell hair accessories or jewelry, or maybe even a little juice counter. I should send an e-mail to the women in the Businesswomen

Unite group, to see if they know anyone. I wonder how much space a jewelry shop or a juice counter would need."

"Not too much," Brooke said, after taking a swallow of water. "Because we still need room for the Sparkle Spa."

Mom nodded, but didn't say anything. Aly worried. What if her idea meant that Mom had changed her mind from the other day and there wouldn't be room for the Sparkle Spa anymore?

She sent a Secret Sister Eye Message to Brooke: *Did I just mess up?*

Brooke sent one back: *I hope not.*

Aly hoped not too.

four
Orange Juice

Auden Angels Day at the Sparkle Spa was always on Tuesdays. Well, it wasn't *just* Auden Angels Day—other kids could come to the spa then too—but it was the day that the Auden Angels came for their rainbow sparkle pedicures. Ever since September, the sixth-grade soccer team had made appointments to have their toenails polished all through the fall outdoor soccer season and the winter indoor soccer season. Anjuli, the goalie, had her fingernails done too. There was usually space for a few other kids to make appointments, but not many.

After school, Aly, Brooke, Charlotte, Lily, and Sophie met to walk to the Sparkle Spa. In order to get there faster, the girls race-walked, propelling themselves forward with their elbows, just like they'd seen people do when they watched the Olympics on TV. Aly and Brooke were expert race-walkers.

"So, still no new place?" Charlotte huffed, trying her best to keep up.

"No," Brooke answered. "But Mom's going to start looking again tomorrow. She might want another business to share the space with True Colors."

"Like the Sparkle Spa?" Sophie asked.

Aly shook her head. "Like a grown-up business," she said. "But the Sparkle Spa will have room there too."

"We hope!" Brooke said, her hair bouncing.

"What do you mean, you hope?" Lily asked.

"Even though Mom said the other day there would be room for us, last night at dinner she didn't guarantee a space. We're a little nervous, but we're trying not to be."

Lily stopped race-walking, pausing right in front of Baby Cakes, a kids' clothing and cake store. "Are you saying what I think you're saying? The Sparkle Spa might close?"

Aly stopped too. "We don't *think* so, but we just don't know for sure."

Brooke stopped next to her sister. "And until we know something for sure, we decided not to worry about it. Right, Aly? Because it might be a waste of worrying."

Aly nodded. Though the truth was, she *was* still worried.

When the girls reached True Colors, they said hello to all the manicurists and the regular customers they knew, like Mrs. Franklin. Her dog, Sadie, was a pet model and had just gotten cast in a TV commercial for medicine that treated allergies. Mrs. Franklin was very excited about it, and the girls were too.

"So we'll be able to see Sadie on TV?" Brooke asked. "That's the coolest ever. Do you think maybe Sparkly could be on TV one day?"

Aly and Brooke's dog Sparkly was very sweet and very tiny, but he was not a dog model at all. Mostly he hung out in his corner of the Sparkle Spa when the girls were at school. Joan had made a deal with the girls' mom that she would walk him during the day. The girls loved Joan for it. Sparkly did too.

"Maybe," Mrs. Franklin told Brooke. "But it's a lot of work, getting your dog on TV, and a lot of training."

Brooke scrunched up her face. She did not like training Sparkly. Pretty much all he knew how to do was "fetch" and "lie down." One afternoon she'd tried teaching him "shake hands," but it hadn't worked out very well.

The girls headed into the Sparkle Spa, where Mom had celery sticks, peanut butter, and water waiting for them. They ate their snack and did their homework—one of Mom's rules—and then opened the Sparkle Spa for business.

Jenica, the Angels' captain, arrived first with Bethany and Giovanna. Jenica and Bethany jumped into the pedicure chairs, and Giovanna sat near them.

"Is it okay if I pet Sparkly?" Giovanna asked.

"Sure," Charlotte told her. "He likes when you scratch his ears."

"I heard your mom might be moving her salon," Jenica said. "My nana told me."

Aly turned on the water in the pedicure basin and looked up at Jenica. "That's the plan," she said.

"We're hoping that means we get a bigger Sparkle Spa," Brooke said. "But we don't really know."

Jenica nodded. "You should see if you could get three pedicure chairs, if you do."

On Aly's list, she'd had written *four pedicure chairs*, just in case another manicurist started working at the Sparkle Spa. But three pedicure chairs would be really nice too, Aly thought. At least then she, Brooke, and Sophie could do pedicures at the *same* time—with no clients waiting.

Aly was in the middle of removing Jenica's old toenail polish when someone knocked on the door. Charlotte headed over with her schedule clipboard. All the people who worked at the Sparkle Spa had special jobs, like in a real business. Charlotte was officially the COO—chief operating officer—of the Sparkle Spa. That meant she was in charge of schedules and lots of other chores that involved organizing.

"Oh," Charlotte said when she saw who was there. "Hi, Suzy."

"Hi," Suzy replied. "Brooke and Aly's mom said I could come back here while she talks to my mom." Then she sniffed the air a little bit. "Nice job covering up the dog smell in here. It's usually worse."

Brooke stood up with a bottle of Under Watermelon polish in her hands—one of the colors in the rainbow sparkle pedicure. "For the last time," she said to Suzy, "the Sparkle Spa does not smell like dog!"

Suzy nodded. "That's what I'm saying. It smells better today."

Brooke huffed and knelt back down to paint Bethany's toenails.

Aly sniffed the air. She thought it smelled a little bit like vanilla and wondered if Mom or Joan had sprayed perfume or something else in the room while the girls were at school.

"So, what's your mom talking to Mrs. Tanner about?" Lily asked Suzy. Lily was stationed next to the sparkly teal strawberry that was the Sparkle Spa's donation jar. Mom wouldn't let the girls charge for their services, but she allowed them to put out a donation jar. Once she took out the cost of the nail polish and other supplies, she told the girls they could donate the money to whatever charity they wanted. So far they'd donated to lots of places, including the pet adoption center where they'd gotten Sparkly.

Since Lily was really good at math, she was the CFO—chief financial officer—of the Sparkle Spa. That meant she handled all the money and reminded clients to donate.

"Aly and Brooke's mom sent an e-mail to a bunch of women who run businesses, including my mom, asking if anyone wanted space in her new salon. My mom's business is mostly online, but she liked the idea of having a *real* store with lots of storage for her supplies, so she came to talk to Mrs. Tanner. If it works out, then I'll get to have Suzy's Spectacular Makeup there too."

"Really?" Brooke asked. "Your mom said that?"

Suzy picked up a bottle of Orange Juice polish. "Not exactly," she said. "But it's only fair. If your mom can give you a space to run a business, my mom can too."

Aly and Brooke sent a Secret Sister Eye Message to each other: *She doesn't know what she's talking about.*

Aloud, Aly said, "That would be nice."

"What kind of business does your mom run, anyway?" Bethany asked as Brooke went back to giving her a pedicure.

"Personalization," Suzy said. "Like if you want sweatshirts with your name on them, or aprons with a company's logo on them, or pencils, or whatever.

She helps you make them, and then sends them to your house."

"Oh yeah," Giovanna said. "My nonna bought hats from her when my whole family went on vacation together. They were really cool."

"All her stuff is cool," Suzy said. "So hopefully she'll get a store, and then I'll get a store, and it'll be great."

"Totally," Giovanna agreed.

But Aly wasn't sure. She wasn't sure about a lot of things:

- *Whether it would be great if Suzy's mom rented out space in True Colors.*
- *Whether that would mean Suzy would get her own space in True Colors.*
- *And whether it would be great—or not—if she did.*

But Aly tried to remember her promise to Brooke that she wouldn't worry until there was something serious to worry about. So she kept quiet and continued polishing Jenica's toes.

five

Very Cherry

Guess who's taking today off?"

Mr. Tanner, Aly and Brooke's dad, opened the blinds in the girls' bedroom on Saturday morning, letting the sun stream in. During the week, their father traveled for work, so when the weekends came and he was home, it was always a little exciting.

Brooke reached for her Very Cherry–colored glasses. She had lots of different-colored glasses so she could match them to her outfits.

Aly rubbed her eyes.

"Mom!" he said, answering his own question. "Joan will run the Sparkle Spa today, and we're going to have a family day at Frankie's Fun Fair. So let's get going."

Brooke jumped out of bed at the words "Frankie's Fun Fair." "We're going to Frankie's?" she asked. "Really?"

"Really," her dad said. "But it's a bit of a drive, so brush your teeth and put on some clothes as quickly as you can."

Brooke raced to the bathroom. Aly rubbed her eyes again and got out from under the covers. "How come we're going to Frankie's?" she asked. She was excited too, but going to Frankie's wasn't a regular weekend activity. The last time they'd gone was three months ago when Dad's college roommate came to town with his three sons.

"I thought the family could use some fun," Dad said. "That's all. Come on, up and at 'em."

After dropping Sparkly at True Colors with Joan, the Tanner family headed to Frankie's, singing along to the radio, even when Dad didn't know the words.

"You mean she's not saying 'I'll get the weather'?" Dad asked.

Brooke laughed at him. "It's 'forget forever'!"

Aly laughed too when Dad scratched his head and said, "Well, that *does* make a little more sense."

When they got to the amusement park, each Tanner chose a ride for the whole family to go on.

Brooke loved the pirate ship that swung them back and forth, making her scream.

Aly picked the swings because it almost felt like she was flying.

Mom chose the carousel because the carved wooden horses' colors were just like nail polish.

Dad picked the Ferris wheel, so they could all see the entire park below.

"This is the best," Brooke said while they were sitting together, swinging in the Ferris wheel car.

Aly agreed but was still thinking it was weird that they were having this family day. Maybe her parents thought they needed to "store up" some happiness because something bad was going to happen.

It turned out Aly wasn't all that wrong.

When the Tanners sat down for lunch—sharing pizza and cheese fries and nachos, which was the exact sort of food Mom didn't like them eating that much—Mom said she had news to share.

"What?" Brooke asked, dipping a french fry in extra cheese.

Mom took Dad's hand. "True Colors is going to move!" she announced. "And I decided to take the larger space you girls liked, the one that used to be a hair salon."

Mom paused and looked at Dad. "I've also decided to ask Carolyn Washington to have her shop in there too. Suzy Davis's mom."

"Wow," Aly said. Her stomach flipped a little. "When is the salon moving?"

"Probably the end of the month," Mom answered. "We need to do construction first, to build a space for Carolyn."

"And for the Sparkle Spa," Brooke said. "Right? A big beautiful room with a window for the Sparkle Spa?"

Mom sighed. "I have to talk to the architects," she said, "and Carolyn. To make sure we have enough space. She needs a lot of storage for sweatshirts and T-shirts and aprons and pencils and buttons and key chains. It's amazing how many items you can ask to personalize on her website."

Aly's stomach flipped again, and all of a sudden she wished she hadn't eaten so many nachos.

"So . . . there might not be a Sparkle Spa anymore?" Aly asked. She looked at Brooke, who already had tears shimmering in her eyes.

Mom ran her fingers through her hair. "I'm going to do what I can. But if it doesn't work out, you girls had a great run. You ran your own business for months, and did a great job."

Aly was finding it hard to breathe. Mom couldn't take away the Sparkle Spa! Not after all the work they'd done building it up.

"But we want to keep running our business!" Brooke wailed. "For*ever*! Or at least until high school! We love the Sparkle Spa. And we have customers who count on us, like the Auden Angels. What would they do if we didn't give them pedicures every Tuesday? They need us!"

"Your mother said she'll try, Brookie," Dad said. "She doesn't want to take away the Sparkle Spa from you, but she has to do what's best for our family. That means being smart about her business plan, finances, and space in True Colors."

Dad asked if anyone wanted to go on more rides that day, but the girls didn't feel like having fun anymore.

Brooke and Aly went straight up to their room once they got home. First they called Charlotte, then Lily, and then Sophie, and told them they needed to have an emergency meeting using their computers.

"Oh no!" Lily cried when they could all see one another's faces on-screen. "This is terrible news."

"It's not a definite no to the Sparkle Spa," Sophie said quietly. "I think it might be okay."

"I think we should write letters," Charlotte said. "And get our customers to write letters too. Then your mom will see how important the Sparkle Spa is to everyone, and hopefully she'll make sure that there's Sparkle space in the new salon."

Aly nodded. "I like that idea," she said.

"Me too!" said Brooke.

"Okay," Charlotte said. "I'm on it. We should all write our own letters first, but I'll get Caleb and he'll help me spread the word. Don't worry, we're going to prove to your mom that the Sparkle Spa is the awesomest kid salon there is."

After they all logged off, Aly felt better than she had since lunch. She sat on her bed to write her own letter to her mom.

Brooke asked to borrow one of Aly's favorite feather pens and did the same.

Would a letter-writing plan really change their mom's mind? The sisters had to try.

Six
Green Beans

That night, Brooke and Aly both slipped their letters under their parents' bedroom door.

Aly's letter said:

Dear Mom,

Please make sure you can find a way not to close the Sparkle Spa. Brooke and I—and Charlotte and Lily and Sophie and sometimes Caleb—have worked really hard to turn it into a good business.

And we've helped a lot of people with all the donations we've made.

So many kids at school love the Sparkle Spa. The Auden Angels think that our pedicures give their feet superpowers—remember they won the championship last year?

Please, think about it again to see if there's room for us. Girls have made friends at the Sparkle Spa, and it makes everyone—especially Brooke and me—really happy.

We don't want the Sparkle Spa to die.

Love,

Aly

Aly had cried a little bit while she wrote the letter. Especially the last linc. She really didn't want the Sparkle Spa to die.

Brooke's letter said:

Dear Mrs. Tanner (I'm calling you that because I'm SO MAD at you that I don't want to call you Mom),

Please, please, PLEASE don't close the Sparkle Spa! I'm so proud of everything Aly and I have done there. I'm friends with so many kids—especially sixth graders who probably wouldn't have talked to me otherwise. And I even learn math every time I organize the nail polish bottles. Aly and I are such a good team—we're not just sisters now, we're business owners, and it's SO MUCH FUN. Also, we donated so much money to good places because of the Sparkle Spa. We're not just helping ourselves, we're helping tons of people and the shelter animals! Please, please, PLEASE make us space in your new salon! If you don't, I'll be mad at you FOREVER.

Sincerely,

Your daughter who is SO MAD at you, Brooke

Brooke did not cry when she wrote her letter. She was just madder than she'd ever been.

"Do you think Joan can help us?" Brooke asked while the girls were getting ready for bed.

"Maybe," Aly said. "But I think it really depends on the space and if there's enough of it."

Brooke sighed. "That salon was really big, though. How much room do you think Suzy's mom really needs?"

"I don't know, Brookester," Aly said. "We'll just have to wait and see."

The next day, the girls opened the Sparkle Spa. Every kid who came for an appointment wrote a letter and left it with Mrs. Tanner on their way out through True Colors. Then other kids who didn't have appointments came by to drop off letters. By the end of the day, the girls' mom had twenty-three letters.

The day after that, more letters came.

And the day after that, even more.

"I have to say," Mom said to the girls when she was driving home on Tuesday night. "Your clients really love you."

"I know," Brooke said. "Because the Sparkle Spa is the best, and that's why you can't close it." She was staring out the window, refusing to look at their mom.

"Will it help?" Aly asked. "That all our clients love us?"

Mom sighed. "I'm doing what I can . . . ," she said.

Aly felt her stomach drop. That wasn't the answer she wanted.

The next day, at recess, Charlotte was sitting on a bench in the playground holding a Green Beans–colored sign that said: HELP SAVE THE SPARKLE SPA! WRITE A LETTER TO MRS. TANNER! PENS AND PAPER AVAILABLE! Aly and Lily were sitting with her.

"Hey, what's going on?" a sixth grader named Daisy asked. She and her sister, Violet, had come to the Sparkle Spa lots of times, but Daisy had been out sick with an ear infection for a few days.

After Charlotte explained, Daisy sat down and wrote a letter on the spot and handed it to Aly. "I'll ask my sister to write one too," she said. "And I'll tell her to give it to Brooke." Violet's classroom was right next to Brooke's.

"Thanks," Aly said. "That's really nice, and helpful."

Suzy Davis had walked over in the middle of the conversation.

After Daisy left she said, "Is it really helpful? Is it changing your mom's mind? Because my mom said she doesn't think there's space for my makeup store either. And I think they need to make space for us both."

Aly shrugged. "I don't know if it'll matter," she said. "But it can't hurt, that's for sure."

Suzy scootched Lily over a little so there would be room for her on the bench, and then sat down. "Maybe you need more than letters," Suzy said.

"Like what?" Lily asked.

"I'm going to think about it," Suzy answered, and got up.

"Are we going to like what she plans?" Charlotte asked after Suzy had left. "I always get worried with her."

Aly tucked Daisy's letter into the back pocket of her jean shorts. "Well," Aly said, "the good news is I don't think anything could make things worse for the Sparkle Spa."

After school the next day, the girls walked over to True Colors with Lily to give their mom more letters. And that's when they discovered what Suzy's idea was. She was standing in front of True Colors holding a huge sign: SAVE THE SPARKLE SPA! it said in sparkly glitter paint. Suzy's little sister, Heather, was holding a sign too that read: MAKE ROOM FOR THE SPARKLE SPA! They were marching back and forth in front of True Colors.

"What do you think?" Suzy said when the girls walked over. "Nice, right?"

"*Very* nice," Aly told her.

"Great sparkle paint," Brooke added.

"I hope it works," Lily said.

The girls walked into True Colors, where Joan stopped them before they could hand the packet of letters to their mom. "I just wanted to let you girls know, I've been working on your mom," she whispered. "I told Suzy too. We *can't* let the Sparkle Spa close."

Brooke threw her arms around Joan, hugging her tightly. The rest of the girls nodded. And for the first time in days, Aly started getting her hopes up. With Joan and Suzy and all of their clients helping them out, Mom *had* to find a way to keep the Sparkle Spa in business . . . didn't she?

Seven
Shimmy Shake

By Saturday, Suzy and her sister had marched in front of True Colors with their signs for three days straight. And they weren't alone: Fourth graders Zorah, Eliza, and Hannah joined them. So did Annie and Jayden, who brought their dog. The whole soccer team came dressed in their soccer uniforms, but wearing flip-flops instead of cleats to show off their pedicures. Mom also had a stack of more than fifty letters! Aly was amazed when Auden Elementary School's assistant principal, Mr. Amari, gave her a letter for her mom too.

"I just wanted to add my support for the Sparkle Spa," he said.

Aly made sure that letter was at the very top when she'd given them to her mom on Friday. But Mom hadn't said a word. Not yes, not no, not anything. So Brooke hadn't said a word to her—not in three days. That's why, on Saturday morning, Aly had to do the talking for both of them.

"Do you girls want to see the new space for True Colors?" Mom asked. "We're in the middle of renovations, and I have to check on a few things."

Brooke stared out the window of the girls' bedroom.

"No thanks," Aly said, looking up from her book, *Jacob Have I Loved*.

Mom pressed her lips together. "I think you girls would really like it," she said.

Brooke sent Aly a Secret Sister Eye Message:

Until she tells us we can have the Sparkle Spa in the new place, I'm keeping up the silent treatment.

"Um," Aly said. "I'm having a good time reading my book. And Brooke's having a good time . . . looking out the window."

"Well," Mom said, "Dad went to the grocery store, and I can't leave you girls home alone. You're going to have to come with me."

Aly was confused now. Going to the grocery store didn't take very long—Dad would be back soon. And Mom had left the girls home alone for short periods of time before.

"Why do we have to come?" Aly asked. "Can't you just wait for Dad? Or leave us alone until he gets here? He'll be home really soon."

Mom closed her eyes. She did that whenever she was trying not to be mad. "Girls, please come with me. It would mean a lot to me."

Aly looked at Brooke. Brooke looked at Aly. They nodded at each other.

"Okay," Aly said, sighing as she stood up. She marked her place with a bookmark. "We'll come."

Aly was actually pretty impressed Brooke had managed to not speak to their mother for so long, since Brooke was a champion talker. Of course, she talked to Aly a lot. And their friends. And even Suzy Davis. And Joan. But just not to Mom.

When they got in the car, Aly said, "So . . . did you read all the notes from our clients? And from Mr. Amari?"

"I did," Mom answered.

"What did you think?" Aly asked.

"I think you girls are terrific businesswomen who have really loyal customers," Mom said. "And that's wonderful."

Brooke exploded. "Does that mean we get to keep

the Sparkle Spa or not!" She couldn't hold her words in anymore.

Mom didn't answer Brooke. By that time they had arrived at the new True Colors location, and the girls followed Mom toward the new salon.

"It actually looks really nice," Brooke sighed. "I love the new sign." It looked like the old True Colors sign, but was bigger and brighter. The letters were glowing, and they shimmered, like the pearlescent polish called Shimmy Shake.

Mom smiled as she unlocked the door.

"Hello?" she called.

The woman in charge of the salon's construction came over. She wore a bright blue hard hat with stickers on it. "So great to see you, Karen," she said. Then she turned to the girls. "You must be Aly and Brooke. I'm Sawyer."

"She's got the best hat on," Brooke whispered to

Aly. "It's the same color as Blue Skies. I love how she decorated it."

"Karen, I have to show you the new sinks. Over here, please."

Sawyer led the way toward the back of the salon and opened a door.

Brooke and Aly gasped.

WELCOME TO THE SPARKLE SPA!

The words were stenciled on the back wall—big, bright, and beautiful.

"So, I need to know what colors you girls want in here on the other walls," Sawyer said, grinning. "And then I can get my team to start painting."

"*What?*" Aly said.

"Oh my gosh!" Brooke squealed. "Oh my gosh, oh my gosh, oh my gosh!" She turned to hug her mom, and Aly joined in the embrace.

"You gave us the best salon ever!" Brooke said. "Why didn't you tell us?"

Mom rubbed her hand across her forehead. "At first I wasn't sure if it was even possible. But yesterday afternoon, Sawyer figured out how to make the space work. We're going to build a loft for Ms. Washington to store her supplies in, which is the perfect solution. And then Sawyer called me this morning to tell me she stenciled the words on the wall. I figured it was just easier to bring you over and let you see the good news for yourself."

Brooke and Aly beamed at their mother.

"Once I saw how much your clients loved you two, and how important your donations were to our community, I knew we had to figure something out. Joan was on your side from the very beginning. But it's really Sawyer who figured out how to save the Sparkle Spa."

When Mom said that, Brooke ran across the salon to hug Sawyer. Mom pulled out an album from her tote bag and handed it to Aly. "I put all the Sparkle Spa letters in here for you to read. They're really wonderful. I'm so proud of you girls."

"Wow," Aly said. "Thank you so much, Mom. This means everything to Brooke and me. Would you show us around?"

Even though the space wasn't fully finished or furnished, Aly took her mom's right hand and Brooke her left hand as the Tanners walked through the new True Colors, imagining what it would look like when it was done.

When the tour was over, Brooke, Aly, and Sawyer sat down to choose the Sparkle Spa color scheme. The girls decided they wanted all four of their favorite colors: pink and yellow for Brooke, and purple and green for Aly. Sawyer suggested yellow walls with purple trim, green tile on the floor, and pink furniture. The girls loved that idea.

"And," Mom said, smiling, "how about four

pedicure chairs and four manicure stations so you girls have some room to grow?"

"That's . . . that's perfect!" Aly said. "Just what we'd hoped!"

Brooke was walking around the new Sparkle Spa when she stopped in her tracks. "Mom, since we're getting the Sparkle Spa, does that mean Suzy's getting her makeup store too?"

Mom frowned. "That's not in the plans," she said.

Just like Charlotte, Mom was not a fan of Suzy. She still wasn't happy about how Suzy had treated Aly and Brooke when she'd interned at the Sparkle Spa for a week. Mom wasn't sure Suzy could be trusted.

Aly and Brooke nodded, but Aly was thinking about how Suzy had stood outside True Colors for three days holding Sparkle Spa signs. Aly suspected Suzy was doing that just so she'd get her makeup store, but still, she'd supported them. And Aly knew

Suzy would be sad—and mad—to hear she wasn't getting her own space.

Aly glanced at Mom. The letters had helped convince her to find space for the Sparkle Spa. Maybe something else would help convince her to make space for Suzy's Spectacular Makeup.

Aly would have to think about that. Was she really considering sharing space with her ever-since-kindergarten enemy? But in the meantime, she and Brooke had to call Charlotte, Lily, and Sophie and tell them the good news. The Sparkle Spa was in business!

eight
Clouder Than Words

By the next day, word had spread around town, and through the next town too: The Sparkle Spa was getting an awesome new home! So many girls stopped by to say congratulations and share in the excitement that the salon was close to hitting its maximum occupancy limit about eight different times.

"One out for one in!" Lily kept yelling. She had asked Aly and Brooke if she could be the "number monitor," making sure they didn't break any rules, since Caleb wasn't around to do security. Aly and

Brooke were really happy to give her that job, because they sure didn't want it!

The whole soccer team stopped by to say how happy they were that their letters made a difference, and three of them even stayed for manicures. Most of the second- and third-grade Munchkins—and a few Flying Monkeys from the recent performance of *The Wizard of Oz*—came too. Two kindergartners even came in and asked if they could have their toes polished in a rainbow sparkle pedicure, just like the soccer team. It was chaos, but happy chaos.

"Just wanted to say how excited I am for you girls," Mom's regular customer Mrs. Bass said as she poked her head in from True Colors. "I think you should consider a bookshelf in the new space. I'd be happy to fill it for you."

"That's actually a pretty good idea," Aly said. Mrs. Bass was always giving away books that her kids had outgrown. Aly and Brooke had about five or six books each from her, including one Aly really liked called *Matilda* by Roald Dahl.

Brooke nodded and then yelled, "Thanks, Mrs. Bass!"

"What else are you going to do in the new space?" Zorah asked. Sophie was giving her a We the Purple manicure.

Aly and Brooke didn't have a chance to answer, though, because just then Suzy Davis walked through the door.

"I'm really, really happy for you guys," Suzy said, flopping onto a beanbag chair, not sounding happy at all.

"Are you okay, Suzy?" Charlotte asked. Aly was surprised, since Charlotte was the person who got along with Suzy the very least. But Suzy did look pretty bummed.

"I'm glad that the Sparkle Spa is getting a new space," she said. "But my mom told me that Aly and Brooke's mom said that I can't have Suzy's Spectacular Makeup. It's because of how I messed up when I worked at the Sparkle Spa a few months ago."

Suzy was actually quiet for a few minutes. Then she added, "You guys forgave me, I don't know why your mom won't."

Aly and Brooke looked at each other. It's true that Suzy had tried to steal their clients and the soccer team's celebration party. But in the end, it had all turned out fine, and Aly and Brooke had forgiven her. Aly hadn't realized that the client and party stealing was the exact reason for Mom not wanting to have Suzy's Spectacular Makeup.

Aly sent Brooke a message: *Should we try to fix this?*

Yes, Brooke answered.

* * * * *

Later that afternoon, when both the Sparkle Spa and True Colors were closed, Mom and Joan were cleaning up their salon and Aly and Brooke were cleaning up theirs.

"So what are we going to do?" Brooke asked Aly. "About Suzy, I mean."

"Let's make a list," Aly said. Lists almost always helped Aly organize her thoughts. And Brooke almost always had great ideas.

Aly grabbed a marker and a piece of paper of the grayish color of Clouder Than Words nail polish.

First she wrote:

Reasons Suzy Should Be Allowed to Have Suzy's Spectacular Makeup

Then the girls brainstormed.

1) For three days, she marched in front of True Colors with her Sparkle Spa signs, which shows that Suzy is supportive and dedicated.
2) The idea about sharing space was hers from the start, so Suzy is smart.
3) Suzy's makeup booth at the school carnival helped the girls tie the boys, which means Suzy is a good team player.
4) People like Suzy's Spectacular Makeup, so she knows what makes a successful business.
5) Even though she sometimes says mean things, Suzy is usually telling the truth, and telling the truth is good (even if being mean isn't).

Aly read over the list. "Should we delete the last one?" she asked.

Brooke pushed up her glasses and nodded. "Yes," she said. "Maybe that's the best idea."

Aly crossed out number five and folded the list. Then she and Brooke walked into True Colors.

"Mom, Joan," Aly said after she flattened out the piece of paper. "We're so excited about the new Sparkle Spa."

"Yes, we are," Brooke added. "More excited than we've ever been about anything ever in our lives, I think."

Aly smiled. She'd been a little nervous, but Brooke with all her chatter made her feel calmer. Aly cleared her throat. "So we're excited about the new Sparkle Spa, but Suzy's really sad about not being able to open her makeup business. I know you may not believe us, but we want to help her."

Aly saw Joan raise her eyebrows at Mom, who was silent for a few moments. Finally she spoke. "Joan was just telling me how much Suzy has grown over these last months."

Hmmmm, Aly thought, *Joan was talking to Mom about Suzy? Was Joan fighting for Suzy too?*

"Well," Brooke said, "I don't know about that. I don't think she's any taller than she was before. But Aly and I came up with a bunch of reasons we think she would be a good choice to be part of the new True Colors space."

"Here," Aly said, handing Mom the list.

Mom pressed her lips together as she slowly read it.

"Okay, girls," she said. "Since you and Joan are so in favor of this, I'll include Suzy's Spectacular Makeup in the new space under two conditions: One, this is a one-month trial period. If Suzy doesn't behave perfectly for thirty days, she's out. And two, she gets a corner of the Sparkle Spa, not her own separate space. What do you think?"

The sisters looked at each other.

"Okay," Aly and Brooke said together. "It's a deal."

"Mom, can we talk to Sawyer about how to fix the space?" Aly added.

"That sounds like a perfect plan," Mom said.

Aly wasn't sure if she would use the word "perfect," but she was pretty sure Suzy would agree to the plan. And the biggest surprise to Aly was that she really hoped Suzy would say yes. She had kind of gotten used to her and wouldn't mind having her around. Even if Suzy did say practically a million times that the Sparkle Spa smelled like a dog.

But how would Aly break the news about Suzy to Charlotte and Lily? Would *they* still want to be a part of the new Sparkle Spa?

nine

It's a Cele-great-tion

The next week flew by. Aly and Brooke couldn't believe everything that had happened in just seven days.

Brooke got a 93 on her spelling test.

Aly finished reading *Jacob Have I Loved*.

And the girls had pancakes for dinner *twice*.

Also, they found out that there was going to be a separate, beautiful table for the teal strawberry jar in the new Sparkle Spa—the best place to remind everyone to make a donation. That made Lily really happy.

And Charlotte found out there would be a big wipe-off calendar on the wall in the new Sparkle Spa, perfect for keeping track of all the customers. That made her really happy too.

In fact, Charlotte and Lily were both so happy that when they found out Suzy was going to get her own makeup corner, it didn't bother them as much as Aly thought it would.

Still, they weren't thrilled.

"Will she be there *all* the time?" Lily asked. "And will she have to contribute to the donation jar?"

The girls were in Aly and Brooke's backyard, relaxing in the grass as Sparkly ran under and around their legs, yipping and yapping.

"Probably not *all* the time," Aly answered. "And we will discuss the donations with my mom and Suzy's mom. Maybe Suzy can have her own jar for donations. I think that's a good idea."

"What do we do if she's mean?" Charlotte asked.

"Well, she is Suzy, so we'll have to expect some meanness. But if she's *really* mean, we tell our mom," Brooke added. "And then she tells Suzy's mom. And Suzy gets into trouble."

"Well, okay," Charlotte said. "At least we won't have to deal with her all by ourselves."

With the Suzy questions answered, the girls started planning the Grand Sparkle Spa Reopening.

"We need a special occasion manicure, of course," Charlotte said. "And a Color of the Week."

"I've been thinking about this," Brooke said, leaning back in the grass, staring straight up at the sky. "I think we should do a version of the rainbow sparkle pedicure, but with the new colors in the Sparkle Spa: pink, yellow, purple, green, and bright orange, for Suzy's area." Orange was Suzy's favorite color, so the girls told Sawyer to use it for the makeup corner. They hadn't told Suzy, though. They wanted it to be a surprise.

"I like that!" Sophie said. "Maybe the order should be pink, orange, yellow, green, purple."

"Ooh, nice!" Brooke smiled, and scratched Sparkly behind his ears.

"I think so too," Aly added. "How about It's a Cele-great-tion for the Color of the Week?"

"And what about a charity for the reopening day donations?" Lily asked.

"Maybe we can give it to Biggie Bigs?" Charlotte suggested. "You know, that program where older kids help younger kids with their homework after school. Caleb and I used to get that kind of help when we were in kindergarten."

"I remember," Lily said. "I like that idea."

"Or maybe we give it to one of the programs that people started at school for recycling or helping people with sports?" Brooke suggested.

Then Sophie jumped up. "I know!" she said. "Let's donate the money from the first day to a charity that

Sawyer chooses. She helped make the Sparkle Spa so beautiful!"

"That," Aly said, "is the perfect idea. She's coming to the opening, so we can ask her then."

Brooke and Aly insisted on picking up Suzy Davis and taking her to the grand reopening a few days later.

"I could've gone with my mom," Suzy grumped when they went to pick her up. "And I wouldn't be squished in the backseat with the two of you."

Brooke rolled her eyes.

"I kind of like being squished," Aly said.

Suzy gave her such a funny look that Aly started laughing. And then Suzy did. And then Brooke. But after the laughing was over, Suzy seemed bummed again.

"There's something really awesome in the Sparkle Spa we want you to see," Aly told her, wanting to cheer her up, but not wanting to give away the surprise.

"Whoop-dee-do," Suzy said.

Brooke rolled her eyes again, and the girls didn't talk until their dad announced, "We're here!"

Brooke and Aly quickly pulled Suzy out of the car and walked her through True Colors to the back of the salon.

"You can do the honors," Brooke told Suzy.

"What honors?" Suzy asked.

"Just open the door!" Aly said.

"What?!" Suzy practically shrieked. "Did you . . . ? Are you . . . ? Am I . . . ? Is this real?!" She was gazing at a bright-orange-colored wall with SUZY'S SPECTACULAR MAKEUP! in green stenciled letters on it.

"It's real!" Brooke said.

Aly looked at Suzy, who had started crying.

"Are you okay?" Aly asked her, pretty sure that

she had never, ever in her entire life seen Suzy cry.

"I'm more than okay," Suzy said. "I've never been this okay in my whole life. How did you make this happen?"

Aly shrugged. "We have our ways," she said. "And Joan helped."

Suzy walked over to her corner and started checking out the drawers. The cabinet was tall and orange, and it was right next to an orange chair. "This is absolutely perfect for my makeup," she said.

"We know," Brooke answered. "It's exactly what professional makeup artists use."

Mrs. Tanner and Ms. Washington showed up at the door. "What do you think?" Suzy's mom asked her.

"It's . . . it's great," Suzy said. "Thank you so much."

Aly was shocked again. Now Suzy was being polite!

"There's one rule," her mom said. "You have a one-month trial period. You have to be on your best behavior. And even after that month, Mrs. Tanner or I can take your makeup stand away if you aren't treating your clients or your friends properly."

"I understand," Suzy said. "Mom, can we go home and get my makeup? So I can start taking clients at the grand opening?"

Ms. Washington smiled. "Dad and Heather are on their way over with your makeup as we speak."

"Really?" Suzy asked. "Thank you!" she said again.

A few minutes later, the new True Colors and Sparkle Spa were packed with people.

First Charlotte, Lily, and Sophie arrived. Then Heather and Dr. Davis along with the True Colors staff. Soon all the True Colors regulars—Mrs. Howard, Mrs. Franklin, Mrs. Bass, Miss Lulu, Mr. Shu, Mrs. Jackson, Mrs. Amin, Miss

Mallory—walked in, followed by the Sparkle Spa regulars—Daisy, Violet, Annie, Jayden, Zorah, Keisha, Hannah, Eliza, Tuesday, Clementine, and all the Auden Angels.

Joan's husband, Isaac, came too, holding Sparkly. And everyone fit, with no problem from the health department!

Aly looked around. She couldn't believe what she and Brooke had started. It was a business, sure, but it was also a community—a family, really—who loved to have fun, be sparkly, and donate money to help people or places in need.

Brooke stood next to her sister. "The new Sparkle Spa is pretty amazing, isn't it?" she asked.

Aly put her arm around Brooke's shoulder and gave it a squeeze. "It absolutely is, Brookester," she said. "It absolutely, positively is."

How to Give Yourself (or a Friend!) a Grand Reopening Special Occasion Pedicure

By Aly (and Brooke!)

* . * . * . * . * . * . *

What you need:

Paper towels

Polish remover

Cotton balls

(Or you can just use more paper towels)

Clear polish

Pink polish

Orange polish

Yellow polish

Green polish

Purple polish

What you do:

1. Put some paper towels on the floor—or wherever you're going to put your feet—so you don't have to worry about your polish messing up the floor. (Two layers might even be better, especially if the floor underneath is not the kind that's easy to clean.)

2. Take a cotton ball or a folded-up paper towel and put some polish remover on it. If you have polish on your toes already, use enough to get it off. If you don't, just rub the remover over your nails once to get off any dirt that might be on there. (You want your polish to look as smooth and as beautiful as possible. And you don't want to have dirty feet!)

3. Rip off two more paper towels. Roll the first one into a tube and twist it so it stays tube-shaped.

Then weave it back and forth between your toes to separate them a little bit more. After that, do the same thing for your other foot with the second paper towel. You might need to tuck it in around your pinkie toe if it pops up and gets in your way while you polish—you can also cut it to make it shorter. (If you don't have any scissors handy, you can also try to rip it. Or you can go find some scissors. Aly always knows where the scissors are. A lot of times, I forgot.)

4. Open up your clear polish and put a coat of clear on each nail. Then close the clear bottle up tight. (For this particular pedicure, it's a good idea to start with your big toe and then end with your pinkie toe because of all of the different colors we're going to use.)

5. Open up the pink polish. Use it to polish both your big toes. Put the cap back on tight. (I always give the polish top an extra twist so it definitely won't spill if it gets knocked over.)

6. Open up the orange polish. Use it to polish both your pointer toes. Put the cap back on tight. (I won't say it again, but you know what I'm thinking.)

7. Open up the yellow polish. Use it to polish both your middle toes. Put the cap back on tight. (I'm thinking it again!)

8. Open up the green polish. Use it to polish both your ring finger toes. Put the cap back on tight. (And again!)

9. Open up the purple polish. Use it to polish both your pinkie toes. Put the cap back on tight. (And one last time!)

10. Repeat steps five through nine.

11. Blow on all your toes, or just let them dry for a minute or two. Then open up your clear polish. Do a top coat of clear polish on all your toes. Close the bottle up tight. (This top coat helps the colored polish not to chip.)

12. Now your toes have to dry. You can fan them for a long time, or sit and make a bracelet or read a book or watch TV or talk to your friend (or sister! Or brother if you have one of those!) until you're all dry. You can also use a computer or a phone and look up things you can do to help in your

community and read about that while you're waiting. Usually it takes about twenty minutes for toes to dry, but it could take longer. (Which is why we try to find fun things to do while our nails dry. Otherwise, sitting in one place for twenty minutes makes my brain go a little crazy.)

And now you should have a beautiful grand reopening special occasion pedicure! Even after the polish is dry, you probably shouldn't wear socks and sneaker-type shoes for a while. Bare feet or sandals are better so all your hard work doesn't get smushed. (And so you can show off your multicolored pedicure!)

Happy polishing!

* . * * . * * . * * . * * . * *

Candy Fairies

Chocolate Dreams

Rainbow Swirl

Caramel Moon

Cool Mint

Magic Hearts

Gooey Goblins

The Sugar Ball

A Valentine's Surprise

Bubble Gum Rescue

Double Dip

Jelly Bean Jumble

The Chocolate Rose

A Royal Wedding

Marshmallow Mystery

Frozen Treats

The Sugar Cup

Sweet Secrets

Taffy Trouble

The Coconut Clue

Rock Candy Treasure

A Minty Mess

For more Sparkle Spa fun including polls, nail designs, and more visit SparkleSpaBooks.com!